KV-683-817

# Here's a story to share!

Sharing a story with your child is great fun and it's an ideal way to start your child reading.

The left-hand pages are 'your' story pages. The right-hand pages are specially written for your child with simple vocabulary and helpful repetition.

• Cuddle up close and look through the book together. What's happening in the pictures?

• Read the whole story to your child, both your story pages and your child's. Tell your child what it says on his* story pages and point to the words as you say them.

• Now it's time to read the story again and see if your child would like to join in and read his story pages along with you. Don't worry about perfect reading – what matters at this stage is having fun.

• It's best to stop when your child wants to. You can pick up the book at any time and enjoy sharing the story all over again.

*Here the child is referred to as 'he'. All Ladybird books are equally suitable for both boys and girls.*

Edited by Lorraine Horsley and Caroline Rashleigh
Designed by Alison Guthrie, Lara Stapleton and Graeme Hole

A catalogue record for this book is available from the British Library

Published by Ladybird Books Ltd
27 Wrights Lane  London  W8 5TZ
A Penguin Company

2 4 6 8 10 9 7 5 3 1

TEXT © CAROLINE PITCHER MMI
ILLUSTRATIONS © LADYBIRD BOOKS LTD MMI

LADYBIRD and the device of a Ladybird are trademarks of Ladybird Books Ltd

*All rights reserved. No part of this publication may be reproduced,
stored in a retrieval system, or transmitted in any form or by any means,
electronic, mechanical, photocopying, recording or otherwise,
without the prior consent of the copyright owner.*

# Molly Maran
## and the
# Fox!

by Caroline Pitcher
illustrated by Gabriella Buckingham

Ladybird

A speckled hen lived in a barn.

Her name was Molly Maran.

One morning the world was cold
and grey.

"I can't scrat and scratch today, the
ground is too hard," said Molly Maran.
"I'll stay in my warm barn and eat corn."
And she settled on the hay like a speckled
tea-cosy.

Molly Maran.

A sparrow fluttered down.
His *eyes* were shiny as blackcurrants.

"Please can I stay in your warm barn?"
he asked.

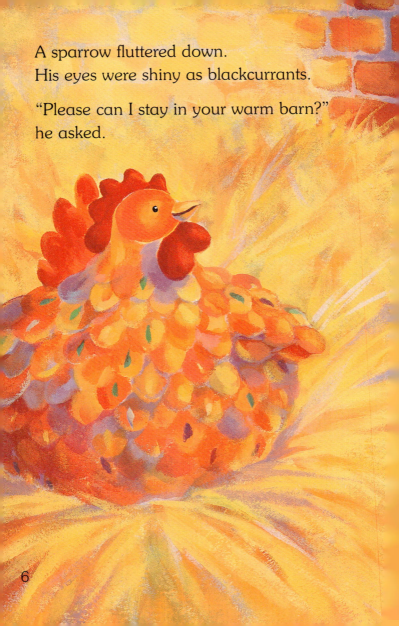

"Can I stay in your warm barn?" asked the sparrow.

Molly Maran put her head on one side.

"Let me think, Sparrow," she said.
"I've thought! Yes. You can stay until the
world is green again."

"You are a kind-hearted hen, Molly,"
said Sparrow.

"Purrk! Puk-puk!" clucked Molly Maran,
and she spun like a speckled ballerina.

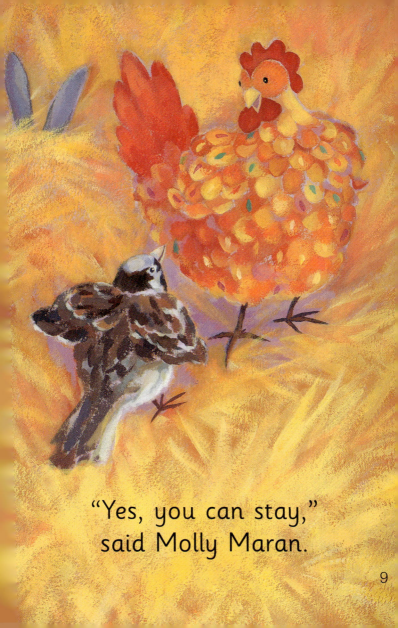

"Yes, you can stay,"
said Molly Maran.

"Oh!" squawked Molly Maran. "I don't remember laying an egg there. What's that? It's got long ears and whiskers!"

Grey Rabbit popped out from under the hay. His nose was as pink as a strawberry.

"Please can I stay in your warm barn?" he asked.

"Can I stay in your warm barn?" asked Grey Rabbit.

Molly Maran put her head on one side.

"Let me think, Grey Rabbit," she said.
"I've thought! Yes. You can stay until the
world is green again."

"You are a kind-hearted hen, Molly,"
said Grey Rabbit.

"Purrk! Puk-puk!" clucked Molly Maran
and she danced on her toes so her comb
wobbled like a red jelly.

"Yes, you can stay,"
said Molly Maran.

13

"All these creatures want to stay in my barn!" she clucked. "I am a Very Important Hen!"

There was someone in the doorway.

It was Dog.

"Please can I stay in your warm barn too, Molly?" he asked. "There's a hole in the roof of my kennel and I'm wet through."

"Can I stay in your warm barn?" asked Dog.

Molly Maran put her head on one side.

"Let me think, Dog," she said.
"I've thought! No, you can't. You are too big
and too rough to stay in my barn."

"Please let him stay, Molly," said Sparrow
and Grey Rabbit. "Remember, you are a
kind-hearted hen."

"I am a Very Important Hen too,"
she clucked. "The Very Important Hen
says no!"

The dog rolled his sad eyes
and slunk away.

"No, you can't stay,"
said Molly Maran.

Now Molly Maran was not very clever,
but she knew she had not been kind to the
dog, and the kind-hearted hen began to
wish she had let him stay.

Ah! There he was in the doorway again!

"Dog! I've changed my mind!" she clucked.
"Dog? You've gone all orange.
Your tail is bushy and your tongue is
as long as a scarf. Why do you look
different, Dog?"

"Because I am not a dog," said the fox
and he grinned like a pumpkin lantern.

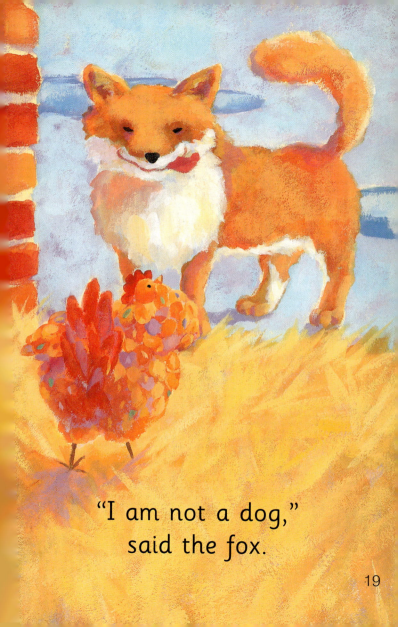

"I am not a dog,"
said the fox.

"You're lucky, Molly Maran.
I'm full of cold curry and custard from
the dustbin. But I will come back later
to your big, warm barn. Back for the
kind-hearted hen!"

The fox turned his wicked eyes away
and slunk out of the barn.

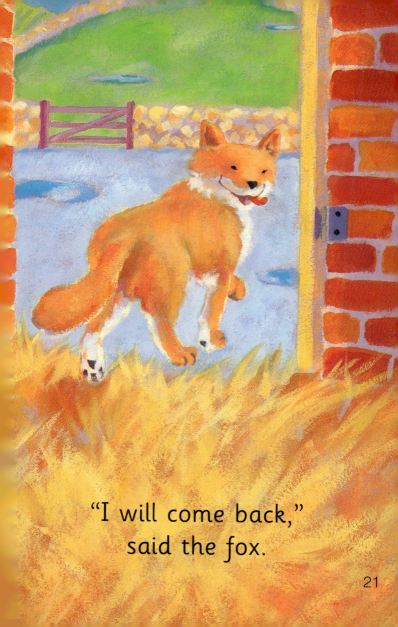

"I will come back,"
said the fox.

Molly Maran squawked, "Purrk! Puk-puk! Oh-oh-oh!"

She dashed out into the big, cold world so fast it looked as if ten legs were running, not two.

There lay the dog with his head on his paws.

"Oh! Hello Dog," she clucked. "Please come and stay in my warm barn."

"Come and stay in my warm barn," said Molly Maran.

"You said I was too big and rough!"
he growled.

Molly Maran put her head on one side.

She said, "Yes. But you are big and rough
enough to keep out the fox. I am a
kind-hearted hen again. Please stay in
my warm barn."

"Thank you, Molly Maran," he barked.
"I'll just get my bone!"

"Thank you," said Dog.

So Molly Maran, Sparrow, Grey Rabbit and Dog all stayed in the warm barn.

The fox did not.

They danced and sang and Molly Maran ate so much corn she thought she might explode.

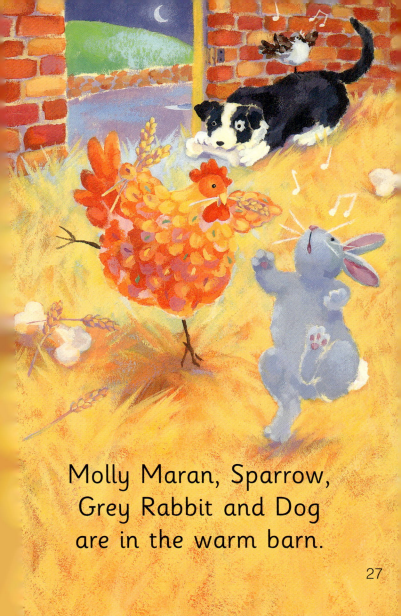

Molly Maran, Sparrow,
Grey Rabbit and Dog
are in the warm barn.

Turn off the TV, close the door, too.
Here's a story to share for just me and you...

## Inky-pinky blot

Who is the inky-pinky blot in the dark, dark pond? He asks everyone who goes by, but no one ever seems to know…

## Caterpillars can't fly!

A baby caterpillar dreams of flying high in the sky but all her friends just laugh. What is she to do?

## By the light of the Moon

Charlie the zoo keeper has gone home and the zoo is quiet. Now it's time for the animals to dance by the light of the moon…

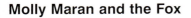

## Molly Maran and the Fox

It's cold outside and Molly the kind-hearted hen says all the animals can stay in her warm barn. But how will she keep out the wily fox?